Mr Mobley and his
Magical Manx Mutt, Max

Story by David Roth
& Art by José Luis Ocaña

To Bettina, Michael and Adam who
are the magic in my life - D.R.

With love to my father, mother
and brothers - J.O.

www.bunchcreative.im

Story and Text Copyright © David Roth, 2022
Illustrations Copyright © José Luis Ocaña, 2022

ISBN: 978-1-8384957-3-2

The rights of David Roth and José Luis Ocaña to be respectively identified
as the author and illustrator of this work have been asserted in accordance with the
Copyright Act 1991.

First published by Bunch Books, Isle of Man 2022.

Book design by Bunch Creative.
Printed by Quine & Cubbon.

Mr Mobley and Max lived in
a tiny **white** house...

under a large **red** wheel...

on a little **green** island...

in a deep **blue** sea.

Every day they awoke to the sound of the giant wheel turning. Every turn drawing the water, which grew the grass, which fed the sheep.

After washing his face, Mr Mobley would stand in front of the mirror and comb his wonderful mustache...

And so would Max.

Then Mr Mobley and Max would have their breakfast.
Banana pudding with just a sprinkle of cinnamon on top.

A quick brush of their teeth and out the door they went
for there was work to be done!

Every morning Mr Mobley would open a big gate to let the sheep run up into the hills where they could eat the grass, lay in the sun and be happy.

Max's job was to watch the sheep to make sure
everyone came home safely at the end of the day.

In the evening after the sheep had been brought inside, Mr Mobley and Max would have their dinner and turn in to bed too.

"Good night Max."

says Mr Mobley.

"Woof."

replies Max.

But then one morning something strange happened.

"Oh no! What time is it Max?"

Mr Mobley and Max did not wake up on time. They did not brush their mustaches and they most certainly did not have banana pudding with just a sprinkle of cinnamon on top...

"Yikes!! We have overslept!!

We never oversleep...
We **can't** oversleep!!
What happened?"

After getting dressed quickly they heard something...
Actually, they heard nothing. It was silent.

Where is the clickity clack?

"Quickly, outside!
Something is most decidedly **not** right!"

"Oh no. OH NO. this can't **be!** Max. quickly!"

"We need to find out what happened.
There is no time to lose!"

"What happened? Are you hurt?
Why aren't you turning?"

"I am sad because the children no longer come and visit me. They used to come all the time. Weekends, summer holidays and even for birthday parties. But if they won't come and see me I shall no longer turn."

"This is no good. No good **at all.**"

That evening Mr Mobley and Max had to make a plan to get the children to return and visit the big wheel, for the island needed the wheel to turn!

Honk Honk. Ring Ring!

Hello all you children, come out now and see,
The wonders that await you with my magical mutt
Max and me!

"Come to the **giant** wheel to see the **magic show!**"

"Boys and girls. it is time for some **magic** and special stunts..."

The children enjoyed the magic show, but now it was time for the grand finale...

Where could Max be?

"Mutton Chops and Cheddar Cheese...
Show me where my dog Max is please!"

Suddenly everyone was silent. The children looked
around for Max. But he had disappeared.

"There's Max!"

At that moment the great wheel began to smile,
which soon turned into a deep laugh.

Then everyone laughed.

That evening Mr Mobley and Max went to bed just a bit nervous. What would happen tomorrow? Would the big wheel turn again? Would the children return?

When they woke in the morning all was quiet. Then they heard a faint sound. As they listened it grew,

louder and **louder** and **louder...**